MW01042399

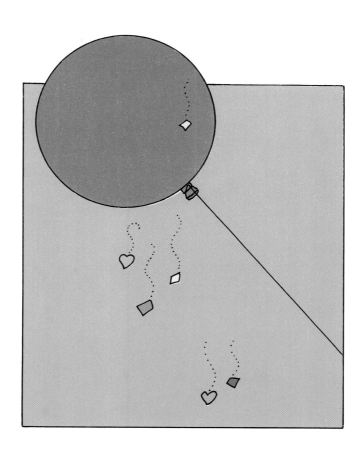

# BY GAIL GIBBONS

HAPPY BIRTHDAY!

Holiday House · New York

For
Bess,
Berton &
Bryce

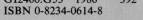

Copyright © 1986 by Gail Gibbons
All rights reserved
Printed in the United States of America

Library of Congress Cataloging-in-Publication Data

Gibbons, Gail.
Happy birthday!

Summary: Examines the historical beliefs, traditions, and
celebrations associated with birthdays.
1. Birthdays—Juvenile literature. [1. Birthdays] I. Title.
GI2460.G53    1986       392       86-297
ISBN 0-8234-0614-8

Everybody has their own special day—their birthday.
It's the date of their birth.

Before calendars were invented, people didn't know the date of their birth.

Finally, when there were calendars, it was easy to keep track of birth dates.

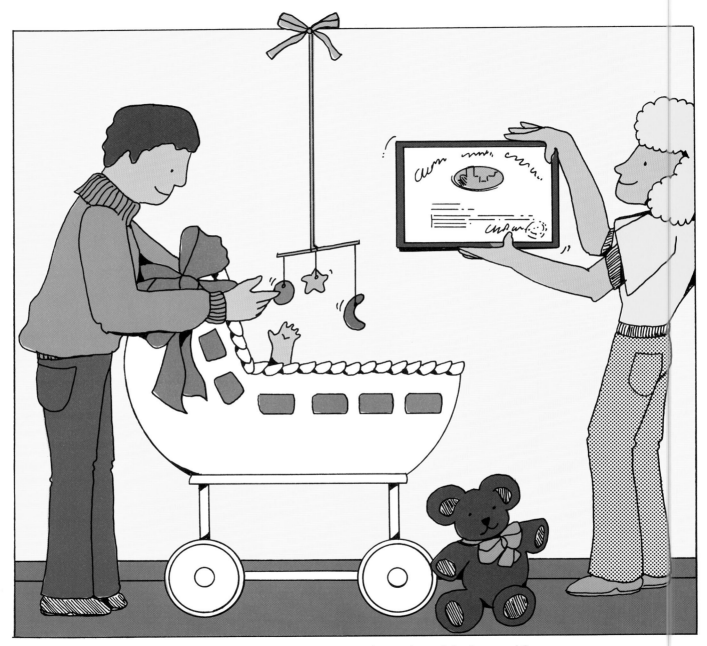

Now, when a baby is born, there is a birth certificate
that has the birth date on it.

From then on, each year the birthday is celebrated.

Long ago people believed that on their birthday they could be helped by good spirits or harmed by evil spirits. They would have friends and relatives around to protect them and make noise to keep the evil spirits away. That's how birthday parties began!

Now birthday parties are for fun!

There are decorations . . .

BIRTHDAY!

and there is a birthday cake.

Many years ago, the Greeks believed there was a
goddess of the moon called Artemis. They celebrated
her birthday by bringing cakes to her temple.
The cakes were round, like the full moon. They were
decorated with lit candles, because the moon glows.

That is why birthday cakes are usually round and have candles on them. Each candle is for one year of life.

At one time people used to think that the smoke from a fire would carry up their prayers and wishes into the heavens.

Now, at a birthday party, a silent wish is made by the birthday person and the candles are blown out in one big puff.

Everybody sings "Happy Birthday." The song was
written in 1900 by Mildred and Patty Hill.

Sometimes the party goers wear party hats and use noise makers.

Birthday cards are given . . .

and birthday gifts, too.

Sometimes games are played.

Everybody has birthday party fun!

January 20 to
February 18

AQUARIUS    WATER CARRIER
You love people.

May 21 to
June 20

GEMINI    TWINS
You like doing
different things.

September 23 to
October 22

SCALES

LIBRA
You are fair.

Some people think that the position of the stars
and planets when a person is born tells what that
person will be like. This is called astrology.

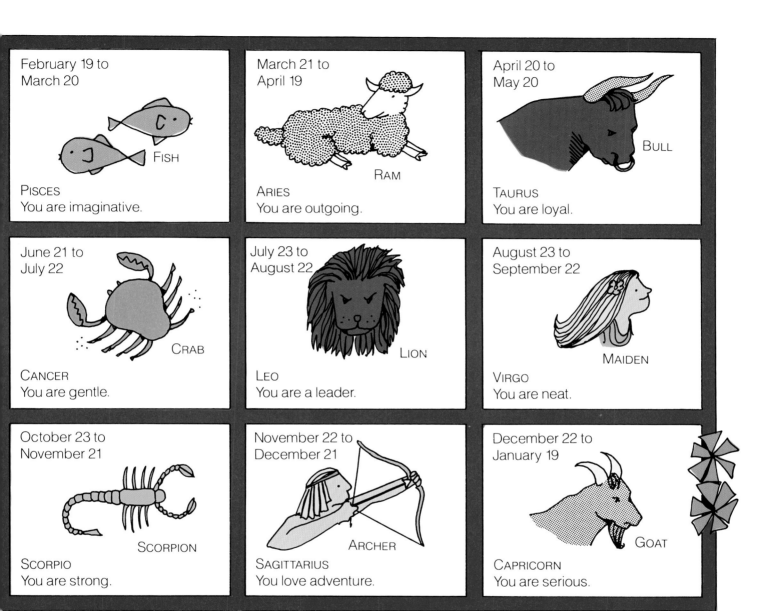

**February 19 to March 20**

PISCES
You are imaginative.

FISH

**March 21 to April 19**

ARIES
You are outgoing.

RAM

**April 20 to May 20**

TAURUS
You are loyal.

BULL

**June 21 to July 22**

CANCER
You are gentle.

CRAB

**July 23 to August 22**

LEO
You are a leader.

LION

**August 23 to September 22**

VIRGO
You are neat.

MAIDEN

**October 23 to November 21**

SCORPIO
You are strong.

SCORPION

**November 22 to December 21**

SAGITTARIUS
You love adventure.

ARCHER

**December 22 to January 19**

CAPRICORN
You are serious.

GOAT

The year is broken up into twelve parts called signs.
The sign that includes a person's birth date is
supposed to tell what the person is like.

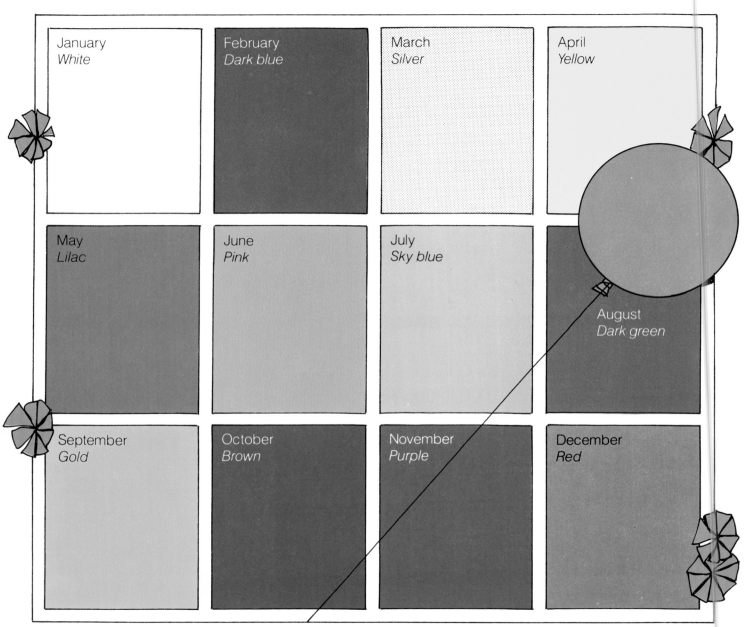

| January *White* | February *Dark blue* | March *Silver* | April *Yellow* |
| May *Lilac* | June *Pink* | July *Sky blue* | August *Dark green* |
| September *Gold* | October *Brown* | November *Purple* | December *Red* |

Over the years, each month of the year has been given a
good luck color . . .

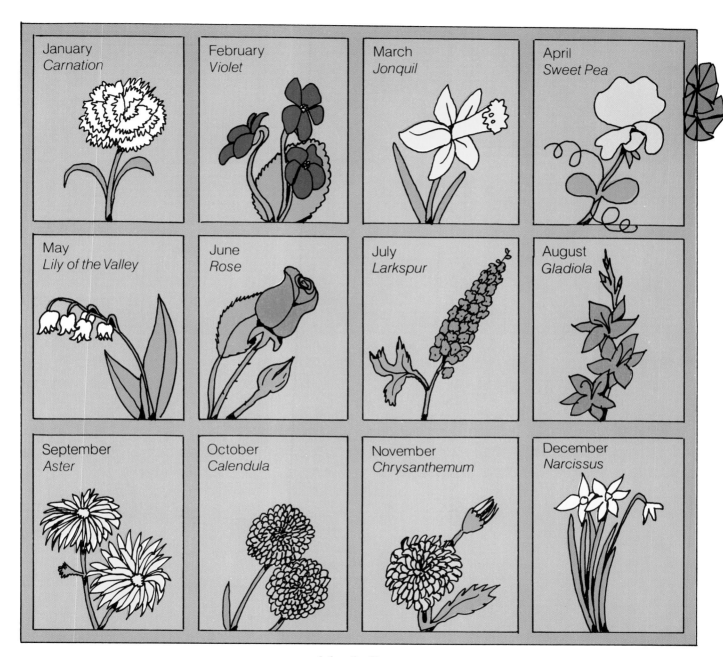

| January *Carnation* | February *Violet* | March *Jonquil* | April *Sweet Pea* |
| May *Lily of the Valley* | June *Rose* | July *Larkspur* | August *Gladiola* |
| September *Aster* | October *Calendula* | November *Chrysanthemum* | December *Narcissus* |

a good luck flower . . .

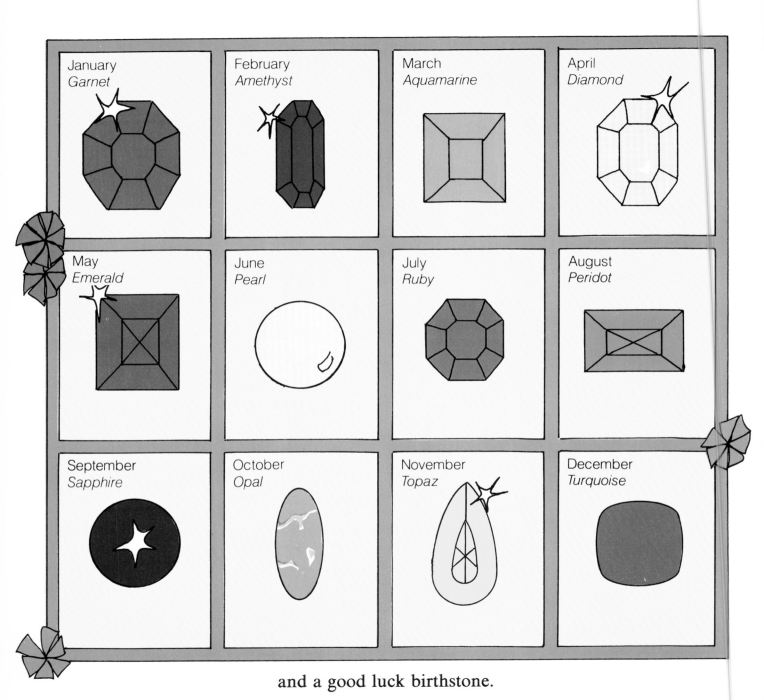

and a good luck birthstone.

Some birthday gifts are good luck flowers or jewelry
with birthstones.

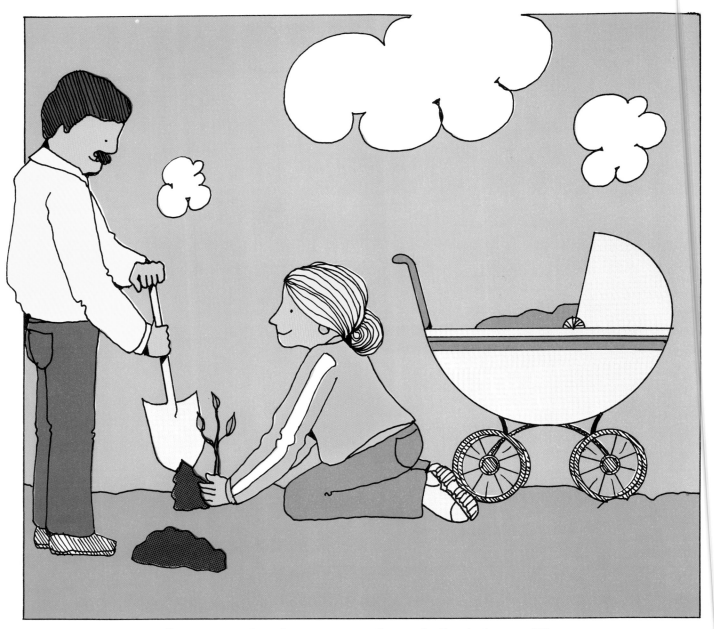

Some people plant a tree after a baby is born. The tree is planted in memory of the special day.

Over the years the tree grows and grows.

But best of all, there is always one special day—
it's your birthday!

| DATE | | | |
|---|---|---|---|
| | | | |
| | | | |
| | | | |
| | | | |
| | | | |
| | | | |
| | | | |
| | | | |
| | | | |
| | | | |
| | | | |
| | | | |
| | | | |